Dedication

To my dad, Steven Lumbert, who taught me to
do the right thing, regardless of the cost.

*The road to Hell may be paved with good
intentions, but that doesn't mean the best
intentions can't lead you to Heaven.*

Contents

Chapter One: Suspicious Suicide...........................5

Chapter Two: Brody's Wake 15

Chapter Three: Party-Cashing Politico............. 25

Chapter Four: Death of a Dwarf....................... 38

Chapter Five: The Mob at My Door 45

Chapter Six: Damant at Death's Door.............. 56

Chapter Seven: Cold Under My Scales.............. 61

Chapter Eight: Fight the Wight 69

Chapter Nine: The Wrongness of It All 76

Chapter Ten: The Dirt on Damant..................... 85

Chapter Eleven: Blindsided 91

Chapter Twelve: Dragon on the Job 96

Chapter Thirteen: Vengeance Interrupted 104

Chapter Fourteen: Good Intentions 111

Chapter Fifteen: The Dragon's a Hero...Again 117

Do you love Vern?.. 126

Acknowledgements.. 127

There's More Fun in FabianSpace! 129

Note on Elvish Names

Runzlykwyndjinxlykbie: Runs Like Wind, Jinx Like Bee. All High Elves have outlandish names, but if you take the time to sound them out, they usually define the elf in question. No one knows why this happens, as the sounding out usually translates into the language of the reader. It's one of God's little mysteries, and a practical joke the High Elves still have not caught onto.

Chapter One: Suspicious Suicide

The late October wind rattled the walls of the warehouse that was my home and the office of DragonEye Private Investigations, reminding me that one, we were in for a rough Colorado winter; two, we really needed better insulation; and three, the cold was probably going to keep us from getting any new cases.

All that added up to a very unhappy dragon—me. My name's Vern, and I'm the dragon half of DragonEye, PI. That's right: a for-real dragon, wings, fire, awesome presence...not quite so awesome thanks to my run-in with St. George, but enough to get the job done.

My job: to find truth through deception, protect the Mundane world from the magical elements they do not understand (but will muck with, anyway), defend the downtrodden of both

Faerie and Mundane, and eventually afford a warmer lair.

I had decided to leave the phone calls to my partner, Sister Grace, and had settled down for a well-deserved nap with my space heater. I heard a crash from the office. I rushed in to find Grace crumpled into a chair, her hands to her mouth, the phone on the floor.

"Guster Brody is dead—and the police say it's suicide!"

I set her phone back on the desk then sat in front of her. Thanks to my post-George size, my head was eye level with hers while I set a paw on her lap.

"You okay?" I asked gently.

Guster Brody was an agent at the Department of Immigrations, one of my least favorite organizations after the Department of Fish & Wildlife. Brody had been one of the good guys, though. He loved the Faerie, and not in the starry-eyed way of someone thinking their favorite fantasy had come to life. No, he actually cared about the people immigrating and did his best to help them get settled. After the fiasco with Addison Lucas, a snotty grade-schooler whose flare for the dramatic almost started an anti-Faerie riot in Los Lagos, he'd done a lot to soothe ruffled feathers—at least on the Faerie side. He was not especially popular with Mundanes.

Even after Addison recanted, her accusations had almost gotten Grace deported for "being a danger to society." Right—Grace (with my help) had banished a monster that Addison and other Mundanes had inadvertently summoned *despite* Grace's warnings, but Sister Grace—a nun, no less—was the danger! Fortunately, Grody had put a stop to that.

We owed him a lot. He was also the first to welcome Grace to the parish choir after she'd found the courage to sing again. His wife was a shrew who never attended church except for special occasions, but Guster and Grace had been good friends.

Grace shook her head, not in answer but in negation of what she'd heard. "I don't believe it, Vern. I won't. Guster isn't like that. Wasn't like that. He was a good Catholic, but more than that, he was a man with a mission. He turned down a transfer because he didn't want to abandon us. He'd never abandon us like this."

"You want to go check out the scene?" I asked.

I bit back a sigh when she nodded. In addition to being ill-tempered and snooty, Mrs. (now Widow) Brody hated Faerie and Magicals in particular. Guster had once said it was his fault because he spent so much time at work, but she worked in the DoI, too.

We arrived at Brody's home just as the coroner was bringing in the body bag. As the door opened, I caught a scent of blood and brains. We hadn't been told how Brody had offed himself; now, I knew it hadn't been pretty.

I told Grace as much, and she promised to brace herself for what we might find.

Larena Hanna, a rookie and one of the first centaur cops on the Los Lagos force, stood watch on the lawn with a scowl that spoke of more than ire at getting stuck with guard duty.

When we asked to enter, she gave me a smile full of sweet malice. "Oh, please do! And give my regards to *dear* Missus Brody."

I smirked back. I didn't need to be a detective to know she'd already encountered the lady of the house herself.

Although modest on the outside, the interior of the Brody home reeked of wealth. I have a high regard for wealth well-invested, and the Brodys knew quality. Antiques, original art, even a Mayan artifact I'd have loved to add to my collection...if I were allowed to collect anymore. I paused before one that was a reasonably good likeness of Quetzalcoatl.

Grace smacked my flank. "Focus, please."

"Right. Sorry." I put aside art appreciation time and followed her up the stairs. At the top, I paused.

In a leather chair behind a cherrywood executive desk slumped Guster Brody, a gun still in his hand, and his brains splattered all over the civic awards on display behind him. The precinct photographer snapped photos, inured to the grisly scene.

Grace gasped at the doorway and made the sign of the cross. I wrapped my tail over her shoulder.

Detective Oren Vialpando looked up from the tablet where he was typing in notes. "What are you two doing here? I didn't call you."

"I did." Father Rich of Little Flower Parish said from behind us. He stopped short at the site of Brody's remains, and, with a touch on Grace's arm, led her away from the room and back to the entryway. Vialpando followed, probably intent on shooing us the rest of the way out the door, but Father stopped him.

"And I was called by one of your officers," he chided Vialpando lightly as he settled the stole over his shoulders.

Vialpando huffed through his cheesy mustache. "Ain't no use in Last Rites, Padre. He's dead. Plus, it's an obvious suicide."

"I'm here for Ellen Brody. However, we will not assume Guster's spiritual state at the time of death," Father chided sternly. "Only God understands what was in his heart at that moment, and only God can judge. You know that, Oren."

Vialpando shrugged. "He left a note."

He held up the paper now ensconced in an evidence bag. Two words: *I can't.*

"Can't what?" I wondered aloud. Vialpando shrugged again. It was his usual form of communication around me, along with grunts and insults.

"It can't be a suicide," Grace protested. "I know him. He wouldn't!"

"Who let that thing in here?" screeched a voice that would make a harpy envy.

Widow Brody glared at us from the top of the stairs, her hair perfect, her eyes red, her dress more suited for a telenovela than an average day in Los Lagos, Colorado. She glared at us with enough fire in her eyes to keep me warm for days.

I looked right and left, the picture of oblivious innocence. Why, who could she be talking about?

"I'm sorry, Missus Brody," Vialpando spoke in a tone more suited for calming an angry wife in a domestic dispute than comforting a grieving widow. "They were just leaving."

Grace, however, wasn't about to be so easily put off.

She stepped forward. "Please, Missus Brody. Ellen. Guster spoke warmly of you. I'm Sister Grace McCarthy of the DragonEye Private Investigations Agency—"

Mrs. Brody held up her hand. "You're one of his, aren't you? A Faerie? I suppose Guster helped you get your citizenship. And you?"

She deigned to look my way.

I didn't feel the need to tell her the story of how I got stuck in the Mundane with no real legal rights and no way to go home without violating the command of Church and Faerie State.

"Who me? I'm a just a thing," I replied with malevolent innocence. It was a skill I'd perfected in my many years in the Mundane. I gave her my snarly smile for added effect.

My zing went totally past her. I'd have to work on my aim.

She turned back to Grace. "With all due respect, Sister," she said in a tone that was anything but respectful, "you may think you knew Guster, but he was my husband. He was a disturbed man."

"He was a faithful Catholic. He wouldn't take his own life!" Grace insisted.

Mrs. Brody's face flushed red. She stomped down the steps to the credenza and yanked open a door. She pulled a bottle out and shoved it at Grace. "He was mentally ill! And he has been for some time. He was just starting to get treatment for it and now..."

She paused and caught her breath. For a moment, her eyes swam with unshed tears. Even so, the impression I was getting from her was anger, insult, even, more than grief.

"I think it's time for you to leave," she said with cold dignity.

Grace read the label, her eyes wide with disbelief. She'd had more than a little experience with Mundane psychiatric medicine. "I'm so sorry. Please forgive me," she whispered as she handed back the bottle.

Mrs. Brody snatched it out of her hand and cradled it against her chest. "Just go."

Then without waiting for us to move, she fled the room. I swear I could hear the sweep of the violins announcing her exit.

Grace headed to the car in silence, but I paused beside Larena the Centaur.

"Ellen says, 'hi,'" I said in my best imitation of snotty teenager. I probably should have had more sympathy for the widow, but it bugged me how she seemed more insulted that we Faerie were desecrating her home with our presence than sad that her husband was dead.

Larena, I could tell, felt the same. She put on her Mean Girls face. She visited the schools as part of the DARE program, so she knew the type better than me.

She flipped her mane and smiled over a curled-up nose. "Omigosh, isn't she the sweetest?"

Then she turned serious. "Listen. Some of the others and I have been talking. Guster helped a lot of us, but we don't think we'll be welcome at the funeral, so as long as I had to stand here and 'not defecate on the lawn,' I've been making phone calls. Wake tonight at the Colt's Hoof. Let's see Guster off in style."

"Works for us, but speaking of work: snoop around, would you? With Vialpando on the case, I don't think we'll get much cooperation, but Grace doesn't think this is suicide...and neither do I."

In my centuries of dealing with humans, I've seen a fair number of suicide notes. Long apologies. Short good-byes. Even a manifesto or two. But "I can't"?

What couldn't Brody do?

Chapter Two: Brody's Wake

One thing the Faerie of every species understand better than the Mundanes is the restorative
power of a good wake. The Colt's Hoof all but
shook with energy, noise, and activity by the time
we got there.

As we entered, we were hit by a wave of body
heat and smoke. Faerie don't have the same issues
about tobacco as Mundanes, and I could make out
several varieties of both Faerie and Mundane cig-
arettes and pipe weed—even a good ol' fashioned
Cuban stogie. The voices of dozens of Magicals
and humans talking at all levels of the auditory
spectrum made a dull roar, occasionally punctu-
ated by the crash of glass and shouts from the back
room.

Even in the most diversified towns in Faerie,
you seldom find such a menagerie of creatures
rubbing elbows, trading stories, crying on each

other's shoulders (flanks, branches), and buying each other drinks.

"Three years!" A nyad floated in a tank constructed by the proprietor just for her species and shared her story with a grandmotherly human who clutching a shopping bag of a purse. "For three years, Guster worked on my application. It kept getting sent back for this reason or that... When his boss demanded an environmental impact statement, I was ready to call it a wash, but Guster said, 'Have faith.' And ...well...in two weeks, I'll be having my first performance at Sea World. But now he won't ever see it!"

As she started to cry, the woman dug into her purse for a tissue. When she held it over the water to her, they both burst out laughing.

The leprechauns had plastered the dart board with little notes, each some obstacle Immigrations Officer Brody had overcome to gain a Faerie their work visa or U.S. citizenship. They were throwing darts at them and shouting "Got another fer ya, Brody!" when the dart struck true.

They'd already put away a lot of whiskey and flung more than a few darts, considering the scraps of paper on the dartboard and the condition of the wall beside it. Charlie had to re-plaster every time they came in for a game.

The elves had absconded with a spot by the fireplace where they took turns eulogizing their friend. I wandered over. I hadn't spoken Elvish in a while; maybe I'd jump in.

Runzlykwyndjinxlykbie was waxing eloquent about how Guster had not only helped him immi-grate, but also got him a scholarship as a running back. He was just segueing from how Guster dec-orated his office—simple, almost Spartan, yet welcoming—to the application process itself. I fig-ured he had about another forty-five minutes to go before I would have a chance to cut in.

I noticed they had a couple of pixie waitresses on hand to refill their glasses without having to be asked. Elves are notoriously long-winded; order-ing a drink could take up to twenty minutes, especially during solemn occasions. If they had to pause to order refills, they'd be here a week.

I wasn't interested in hearing about his fresh-man year. I wandered back to Grace, who was just finishing an impromptu prayer with a couple of dryads. From the bar, Bacchus gave me an expan-sive wave of greeting.

Even empyre, the Faerie analog of the gods, had come to pay their respects. Bacchus had stationed himself at the center of the bar, a pair of nyads on his lap while a Mundane woman clung to his arm. Around him, several people of different species drank and laughed at his jokes. Bacchus didn't know Guster, and he certainly hadn't tried to get US citizenship. He just hated to miss a party.

I jerked my head at him in acknowledgement and continued to scan the room.

Neither the coroner nor the widow would have acquiesced to allowing the guest of honor to attend, so someone had rented a casket from a local funeral home.

I grinned, imagining the funeral director's face as someone explained that they didn't want to buy it, just rent it for the night for their dead friend's drinking party.

It sat at the far end of the room, bearing numerous framed photos of Guster Brody posing with those he'd helped to gain citizenship. Larena stood beside it, talking to a Hispanic Mundane who was having a hard time not looking at her chest. Understandable, considering as a half-horse, she stood head-and-shoulders taller than him, but I was sure the traditional silk scarves she wore instead of a blouse didn't help matters.

Despite her casual attire, she had her badge and her taser strapped to her waist. Got to admire someone who doesn't look for trouble but is ready for it, anyway.

She caught my look, excused herself, and wove her way over with a skill that spoke of experience with navigating crowds. "Hey. Glad you could make it. Sister Grace, are you okay?"

A pixie bearing a glass of wine almost as large as she was flew up to Grace and handed it to her, pointing back to Bacchus. Grace took it and raised it in his direction with a warm smile of thanks. She knew him from when she'd studied music with the Muses.

"I'm fine," she told Larena. "Still in a wee bit of shock, and I don't believe for a moment Guster took his own life."

Larena's horsey huff spoke of her frustration. "None of us do. But there's the note, and Widow Brody insists she didn't know he'd bought a gun. She can't imagine why he would; they had complete confidence in their security system, according to her."

"Brody was not a violent man," Grace said. "I can't imagine him shooting anyone, and certainly not himself."

"His were the only fingerprints on the gun," Larena told us. "I suppose, if he was..."

She let her voice trail to silence. Brody had kept his mental state a secret in life; who were we to divulge it after his death?

Grace shook her head, sadly. I knew she was thinking about whatever she'd read on the bottle of pills Widow Brody and shown her. What demons had he been battling?

Larena continued, "Still... It settles wrong on my hide. I sent in McConkey. You know how he's aching to get on the force and out of the mailroom."

I snorted. McConkey was the only pixie on the force. How Brody convinced Captain Santry to take him, I will never know, but I do know Santry's been regretting it ever since. McConkey at first read every report and piece of mail that crossed Santry's desk and eagerly gave a summary and helpful advice until Santry threatened to arrest him. Rumor has it that the police chief has an oat-meal box with air holes knifed into the top that he brings out whenever McConkey starts in with "helpful advice."

Larena shrugged. "I know. But the fact that he's nosey and eager is in our favor. He loved the idea of going undercover. He didn't find anything, but he said the place 'felt wrong.' Nothing he could put his finger on, though. He thought he heard some moaning, but it was probably Mrs. Brody. She's a heifer, but she did lose her husband.

"He wanted to go back tonight, and I told him okay but to stay out of the house and just listen. He should be fine."

She just had to say that.

On cue, McConkey appeared behind her and dropped onto her back, coughing and wheezing. He stank of insecticide.

Larena twisted, trying to see him over her shoulder. "McConkey! What happened?"

"RAID," he gasped.

A shrill alarm rose among the pixies in the room, and two assumed the form of red finches with tiny masks over their beaks. Gingerly, they grasped his arms and carried him to the bar, where other pixies had already filled a bowl with warm, soapy water. Some folks stopped their mournful revelry and gathered around to watch as pixies in hedgehog form scrubbed their contaminated friend.

Obviously, this kind of thing has happened to the diminutive, shapeshifting race on more than one occasion since the Gap had opened between our worlds.

"This is an outrage!" a female pixie hollered. For so small a creature, she had good lungs. Conversations paused...except for Runzlykwynd. He was in The Zone. "We should report her!"

"No!" McConkey pleaded. "Santry will fire me, for sure! It's my fault. I got careless. Someone was there with her. I thought if I looked like a luna moth, I could cling to the window screen and watch. Who doesn't love luna moths?"

"And she just happened to have a can of RAID handy?" the female pixie demanded with a stamp of her tiny foot.

"She reached into the closet. I didn't know what for. Stupid, stupid, rookie mistake."

"Rookie mistake? *Rookie mistake?* Try potentially fatal mistake! What if she'd had one of those zapper rackets or been more aggressive with the spray? You could have been killed!" Her voice grew shriller with each sentence, but unlike the Widow Brody, hers held fear and true grief at the thought of losing her love.

McConkey sighed theatrically. "I know, my sweet petal. I know, and forever will this lesson be branded upon my heart—"

"Brand it in your brain!" she shouted, causing a ripple of laughter.

"Yes, my gentle spring dew. I regret my foolish eagerness and the pain it has given you, and even worse, the anguish it could have caused. I am wiser now, for I will from henceforth weigh each action against the reaction of my wise and caring Templegrass.

"Forgive me, my dear dandelion seed, for the withholding of your love pains me more than the vilest of pesticides."

I wanted to gag. McConkey had a reputation for being over-the-top in everything he did, but this was excessive even for him.

Nonetheless, when he held out his hand entreatingly to his sweet seedy dandelion or whatever she was, everyone sighed. Templegrass rewarded him with such a sickening mix of anger and smitten pride, I had to look away.

As the two cooed lovingly and their audience applauded, I rejoined the elves. Runzlykwynd had just started explaining football. I could say you've never lived until you've heard the American sport described in High Elvish, but in reality, it just feels like a lifetime.

Just as he was explaining an "end run," a bunch of humans decided to crash our party.

Chapter Three: Party-Cashing Politico

The door opened with a bang, thanks to the October wind, and some Mundanes entered. More than some. A half dozen, then a few more. They formed a crowded half circle around the door. There were already some Mundanes among the revelers, mostly immigrants Guster had helped, spouses, or Guster's close friends from the department or church. This new group looked like none of the above.

Around the bar, people—and hackles—rose.

I started for the door, but Larena tapped me on the shoulder, and I held back with a nod, ready to back her up if needed.

Larena walked over, hand on her taser. Despite her filmy attire, she conveyed authority. "I'm sorry, but the bar is closed for a private party."

"Oh, we know!" a boisterous voice, friendly in a plastic sort of way, sounded from just outside the threshold. Trevon Damant, gubernatorial candidate and head of the Los Lagos branch of the Department of Immigration, sauntered through the door and tapped one of his groupies on the shoulder. They parted, leaving him a clear aisle into the bar. I wondered if they practiced that.

Once ahead of his pack, Damant spun around and addressed the crowd. He raised his hands as if in friendly greeting. He reminded me of an old photo I'd seen of a Mundane president named Nixon; all he needed was to arrange his fingers into a victory signal.

There was nothing friendly or inviting in the glares he received from the legitimate attendees. Even so, he spoke as if he'd received a warm welcome.

"Please, my friends, don't let us disturb this solemn occasion. After all, I, too, cared for my hard-working and troubled subordinate. We are here for the same noble reason: to set aside our differences and join together, in all our diversity, for the common purpose of celebrating the life of a man who gave his mind, heart, and soul to the laudable cause of securing freedom and prosperity for the deserving inter-dimensional petitioner!"

Stony silence met his declaration. No one sat down despite the patting motions he made with his hands.

The way he smiled at the crowd, however, you'd think we'd given him a standing ovation. Even so, the smile didn't quite meet his eyes; or maybe it was the Botox. I wasn't close enough to tell and not anxious to get any nearer.

Then I heard the telltale whirr-click of a camera on burst mode. I wasn't the only one. Muttering among the mourners. Larena kept her hand by the taser as she scanned the crowd. Several of her fellow officers had joined her, placing themselves in strategic points between the mourners and Damant and his posse.

Damant had taken over the Department of Immigration seven years ago, and every Faerie knew that any good Brody had done since had been *despite* Damant's "caring" leadership. Many an application was sent back because of minutia like typos or a request for rewording; several were simply "lost in the shuffle." Despite the fact that the United States wanted to encourage the immigration of Faerie, citizenship and green-cards had slowed to a molasses-thick trickle thanks to Damant's bureaucratic "checks and balances."

Finally reading the crowd, he tried a new tactic. He lowered his arms—dramatically, mind you, complete with the shoulder slump I'd seen on cartoons right before the character leans his head against a tree. Trust me; no dryads were going to volunteer for that role.

"I understand. You have no reason to trust me. The process has been difficult for so many of you. I take responsibility for that. I own it—"

"Shut up!"

The crowd stirred, and Balga Shieldforger, a sturdy blond dwarf with tear-streaked cheeks and clenched fists, stomped through to snarl into Damant's downcast eyes. "How dare you soil this wake with your presence? You were no friend to Guster—and you were no help to any of us."

Damant put on his Compassionate Face. "Balga...is that correct?"

"You know cave-in well it is! Do you think we've forgotten how, when we asked for permission for our cousins to join us, you said there were no jobs for 'our kind,' even though we dwarves had reopened your silver mine? How those jobs later went to Mundane immigrants who had their paperwork pencil-whipped because of the employment crisis?"

"Yeah!" came the husky shout of the dwarves in the room.

Each camp surged forward—slightly, more of an attitude than a motion, but enough that the cops made ready to intervene. Grace pushed through until she was behind Balga, but all she did was set her hands on the dwarf's shoulders.

Damant glanced over the crowd, then focused on Balga. "I... I am so sorry if you—"

"Save it! I'm not even going to get into how you threatened us with fines if we didn't take your substandard employees. You!"

She pointed at one man in Damant's group, who jumped to attention.

"Didn't my Urist save you when you nearly buried yourself trying to make a cave a little taller so you didn't have to duck your head? Shame on you for following this man!"

She stared him down until he at last wilted, then gave the last of her murderous glare to Damant.

He sighed. "All right. I see I'm not welcome here. I merely wanted—"

"You wanted to make political points by modeling yourself as the friend of the grieving Faerie. You don't think we recognize slag when we see it? You may be able to convince your cronies that you stand for diversity and opportunity, but we are not stupid. All your talk about opportunity, but you want to give it to those who will help your career. The rest of us are left to fight for our chances—and we just lost our best advocate in the Mundane! Now get out of here and let us mourn in peace!"

The crowd roared its approval, and I could smell as much as see Damant's posse brace for a fight. But the politician raised his hands in surrender, gave everyone a regretful, pitying look, then sighed with theatrical deepness. He was as bad as McConkey and less effective.

The crowd's glare grew even more hostile.

The cameraman started to raise his camera again, but one of the pixies flew in front of the lens. Its wings metamorphosed into large butterfly wings with an obscene pattern. He was joined by two others in the form of wasps.

With a shrug, the guy brought up his hands in true surrender, the camera bouncing against his slight belly on its neck strap.

Perhaps Damant took that as a true sign of defeat. His own arms lowered and spread, he herded his little flock back out of the bar.

The patrons cheered and gathered around Balga, but the dwarf just spun and buried her head into Grace's habit.

"Why did he have to come? Why does that horrible man have to ruin everything?"

One of the other dwarves patted her back roughly. Her words were even less comforting. "You had the right of it, him wanting to use our pain to his advantage."

"Don't worry about that!" one of the pixies said. "I got a cousin who's dating a gremlin. We'll be making sure none of his photos come out, and Charlie's already calling the *Gazette* to tell them all about Damant crashing the party."

"What's it matter?" Balga sobbed. "It's shale against stone. We'll never make it here."

Grace didn't answer but made shushing sounds. "Maybe we should find Urist. Where is he?"

Balga pushed away from Grace and wiped her nose with her sleeve. "In the back, drinking."

The dwarves had taken over the small party room, and trust me, it looked like an invasion. Chairs were overturned, and a small mountain of broken bottles took up one corner of the room, with shards scattered outward from it like a landslide of alcohol and glass. The place reeked of beer.

"Another round!" Urist slammed his fist on the table, making its contents jump. The liquid in the glasses and pitcher sloshed. The harried waitress was nonetheless prepared; she reached through the window that connected the room to the bar and pulled out six more bottles, which she placed in front of each dwarf.

Urist snagged his by the neck and held it up. The others followed. I saw the distinctive black heart over crossed swords on the label. That was good beer. I winced at what was coming next.

"Oh, Blackheart Stout, so roasty and dark, smoky in aroma, your thick head tickles the mustache as the tongue savors your creamy texture. Many a dwarf has thanked the Mundanes who devised this nectar to comfort us after long days in the mine! But our friend Guster Brody cannae enjoy it!"

"So neither shall we!" the others responded.

They pressed the bottles to their chest, then flung them, unopened, into the corner. Glass shattered and beer fizzed. Blackheart Stout did have a nice head.

At the table, the dwarves raised glasses of cold water with lemon.

"Guster, we suffer for you!" Urist declared.

"Suffer!" the rest agreed, and they guzzled the water until the lemon wedges smacked their teeth. Then, they slammed the glasses onto the table and hung their heads.

"I'm so sober," the little one lamented. Must have been his first wake.

After a moment of silence, the next dwarf called, "Another round!"

"Urist," Grace called as the drinks were being set up.

His fist around a bottle of Norm, he twisted and saw his still-sniffling wife standing between us. He left the bottle and hurried to her.

"Balga, my amethyst. What's wrong?"

"While you guys were mourning your way through the inventory, we had a visit from Trevan Damant," I told him.

Urist's eyes widened, and he grabbed Balga by the shoulders. "Tell me you didn't!"

"Of course, I did," she half-snapped, half-sobbed. "Too many years we've been silent while that man has bullied and manipulated us and used his position to further his own ends at our expense. Blackmailing us into hiring his pet immigrants.

"You could have died in that cave in! I could have been throwing bottles for you. It's only your stubbornness and God's grace that let you survive. Guster was looking for evidence. That's why he died—and Damant had the gall to come here and make speeches!"

"Balga!" How a dwarf could hiss a guttural name like that, I had no idea, but he did. It was a talent.

Of course, that didn't distract me from her words so much as highlight them like a cheap neon sign. "What evidence? Did Guster suspect Damant of wrongdoing?"

Urist gave his wife a look as dark as the stout he'd just thrown away, but he answered. "Damant was blocking my cousin Ordon's entry into the Mundane. We needed his engineering skills, but no matter how we explained it, the answer was, 'No.'

"Later, we got a message. No address, but we knew it was from his office. It was a list of names, and the suggestion that if we hired them on, there might be a chance of getting Ordon, too—but if we refused, we would see the mine closed for bad hiring practices. Then, they never followed through on Ordon, but we couldn't fire any of the new workers. Some were okay, willing to learn. Others just wanted to pull in paycheck; and some, dumb as dry wood.

"It was a long time ago, Vern. Just let it be. I don't want any trouble. Balga, we should get back to our hotel. We're going home tomorrow morning." He started for the door.

She grabbed his sleeve. "No, Urist, please. We can't let this continue!"

"Balga!"

Balga clenched her face and her fists, but she huffed a sigh and followed her husband out of the bar and into the cool night.

When Grace and I returned to the party, a soggy but decontaminated McConkey flew to us. "Vern, Sister Grace, I didn't want to say anything while you were busy with the dwarf, but that person I saw with Widow Brody? I'm pretty sure it was Damant."

Grace and I exchanged glances.

"What couldn't Guster do?" she wondered aloud.

You know what they say about great minds. "I think maybe we should mingle and find out what other stories we hear about Guster's caring employer."

I went home with more than one tale of mysterious messages from Damant's office—and a five-gallon bender. The next morning dawned no clearer or warmer than the day before, and added to that, my head pounded. Curse that Bacchus for creating a fountain of ethanol just for me. Curse me for giving into the temptation!

I didn't care how cold it was. I was going to the alley to throw up into a dumpster, and then fly to some big empty area and breathe fire until I burned off the hangover. The owner of a nearby lot had promised me a little money if I burned the weeds for him. I could kill two birds with one stone.

I loved my fire. It's one of the lovely benefits of being a dragon.

I was heading back, chilled but no longer battling a headache, when I spotted Urist running down my street. I landed beside him. "Urist, what's wrong?"

Urist looked torn between the urge to cry and to tear something apart—possibly even me.

"He's done it, Vern! He's killed my beautiful amethyst! My Balga is dead!"

Chapter Four: Death of a Dwarf

The October wind nipped at my scales like Jack Frost's manic terrier, but no way was I going anywhere with Urist ready to fall on his knees in sloppy grief or run the rest of the way to Damant's house in violent rage. Considering the dwarf lacked both his ax and his shoes, I had the feeling grief would win out, but I wasn't taking any chances.

As my dwarf friend babbled incoherently about his beautiful Balga, her life cut from her like useless tailings, and how he was going to get an ax and chop Damant down to size, one body part at a time, I heard the wail of sirens growing closer. I again noted Urist's pajamas and bare feet. Did the police already have their suspect in mind?

I didn't have time to scold. "Slow down—or better yet, speed up but make sense. What happened?"

"I told you, he killed Balga! She...she went for a walk, but she never came home. She's like that, you know, when she gets mad. Used to spend hours wandering the mines. There's no reasoning with her when she's that way, so I went to sleep. This morning, the police showed up, and they said...they said..."

He paused to wipe his eyes with his beard. "She shouldn't have confronted Damant. We all know what he's like. This time, he's gone too far. When I find an ax, I'm going to start with his ankles!"

The police cruiser rounded the corner. Urist gave a start. I snagged him with my tail before he could run.

"Listen to me. Stay still, stay quiet, and trust me. We'll get you out of this, and then we'll find Balga's killer."

Damsels and Knights! Did I just take on a case—for free? My nun partner was rubbing off on me.

"I know who did it!" Urist protested.

"You *think* you know—and so the cops do, it seems. If they're wrong, then you can be, too. Now, be a good, cooperative suspect before you make things worse."

The cruiser pulled up and the cops jumped out, weapons drawn: officers Starkey and Hutchinson, humans, real go-getters on the force, aching to make detective, but by-the-book. I could work with that. Hutchinson had a bruise under his cheek that looked painful. Dwarves have mean uppercuts.

Captain Santry was old enough to have watched 70s police shows. I know he paired them up just to make the joke. How could I miss an opportunity to help out? I launched the opening salvo.

"Hey, Starsky and Hutch! You guys are never going to make detective if you start arresting the grieving widowers instead of finding the real murderers."

Ever the straight man, Starsky-Starkey replied, "He's wanted for assaulting an officer, nothing more...yet. Please step away from the dwarf."

I gaped at the dwarf in question. "They didn't accuse you of anything? But you *ran*? Are you sure all you had last night was lemon water?"

Urist put on a stubborn pout, but Hutch-Hutchinson spoke up. "Officers on patrol found his wife's body in a back alley off East 27th. We were dispatched to inform him and ask him to accompany us identify the body. But instead, he started screaming about killing someone. We tried to restrain him, and he resisted and ran. We've been in pursuit. Now, step away."

Well, at least he wasn't being pegged for murder, yet. "One condition. I want the details of the case. Otherwise, I'll go turn him in myself and ask for a reward. You'll lose your collar, and you can explain how a four-foot, middle aged dwarf got the better of you both. I'll be sure to tell my side of the story with all the appropriate embellishments."

The two exchanged exasperated looks. Guess we were ruining their day. Fine by me. My day, which should have involved making up for lost naptime, was already ruined, and my teeth were chattering. Do you know what it's like to chatter with dragon-sized bicuspids? Not pleasant.

"We'll give you our notes," Starkey compromised. "Anything more, you have to check with the captain."

I could deal with that.

"Go quietly," I told Urist. "Apologize to the nice officer, but don't say anything else. Grace and I will call Gord and get him to pay your bail, then we'll be over as soon as we can."

Gord was Urist's partner in the mine. Urist sighed. "He's going to crunch gravel. We promised we weren't going to make waves. We just wanted to mine..."

By the time they loaded him into the car and I made sure Starkey had e-mailed me his case notes, I was almost too cold to fly. The Medsea (the Faerie equivalent of your Mediterranean) is my natural habitat, with mild weather and warm beaches. When the snow hits the mountains, I would snuggle deep inside my abandoned dwarf mine for a peaceful hibernation for a month or two.

I missed my mine lairs. Dwarves always make a portion of their mines with dragons in mind, so that when the mine plays out and they leave, we can make a home of it. I sometimes wonder if Smaug in Lord of the Rings was simply taking what he thought was his. Then again, Mundanes don't seem to find housing a dragon the honor it truly is.

There's a thought! I wonder if the Shieldforgers can do the same for the mine here? Might make it worth my impulsive pro-bono offer.

When I first arrived in the Mundane, my plan had been to find a nice cave in the mountains to set up residence in. The government put a quick stop to that. They would not let me create a lair on public land and demanded that any Mundane wanting to host a dragon on their own property pay dearly for the privilege. Like the nyad, I was a victim of the "environmental impact study" but I didn't have a Brody to fight for me. Instead, I ended up in the garage of Little Flower Parish until a dying widow willed me a leaky warehouse full of junk. Even that took some fancy lawyering to let me keep.

But that had been a long time ago as the Mundanes count. No one worried about me disrupting the local wildlife anymore, and if the dwarves owned the mine, maybe they could claim cultural heritage.

The thought was enough to warm me on my flight home—or at least make the cold seem less biting. As I came in site of my lair, however, I could see that Urist might have to cool his heels a little longer than I'd expected. A crowd had gathered at our doorstep, banging on the door and shouting.

Chapter Five: The Mob at My Door

I hovered some distance away and took stock of the crowd. I recognized a few faces—good. That meant they were mad about something other than me, most likely. Most were Faerie. Could they have heard about Balga already? Some waved paper in their fists, but regular document stuff, not newsprint. Most people, even Faerie, got their news online nowadays, anyway.

Grace was taking her own sweet time answering. Still, the protection spells around our house were not activated. She was probably indisposed rather than feeling under threat, then.

No point roaring or blasting fire—the crowd was too loud to hear me and hot enough as it was. I dove for the mob, stopping short of their heads with a mighty backflap of my wings. The resulting snap and blast of cool air got everyone's attention. They backed up from the porch to let me land.

Confirmed: They weren't mad at me; what a nice change of pace. Granted, I hadn't seen any pitchforks, but you can't be too careful with angry crowds.

"Please, Vern, you have to help us. Damant's out of control." The nyad from the wake stepped out of the crowd. She wore a thick trench coat over a wetsuit, and I do mean wetsuit. It had been specially designed by a team at CSU-Los Lagos to hold a thin sheet of water over her entire body. It allowed her to move about on dry land, but I could see how she shivered; she was probably in ice water by now.

Damant again? I opened the door, led the way in, and directed them to the kitchen, as there was no way they'd fit in the office.

Now that someone was going to listen to them, the Faerie shuffled in politely. As Runzlykwynd shut the front door, Grace burst in from the interior doors that separated the common kitchen/office area from the rest of our home. She must have been in her workshop.

"What was all that ruckus?" she demanded, then she caught sight of the shivering nyad.

"Coral! How are you out in this weather? Into the shower with you. We have to get you warmed up."

She took the paper from the nyad's hand, set it on the table under my nose, and led Coral through our doors and to the bathroom.

It was a hard copy of an e-mail, saying that, in light of Brody's death, they were reviewing all his case files, and some irregularities had arisen in hers.

I huffed a sigh that rattled the paper and looked up at the expectant crowd. "All of you?"

They slapped down copy after copy, as fast as a speed-reading dragon like me could scan them.

"Lacking an official, paper copy of the birth certificate," said the dryad's. Another expressed doubt that the shoemaker elf could adapt to a technological society—he passed me his letter via an iPad; gotta love the irony. My favorite, by far, was Coral's: Her case was being held for a second study on whether the dolphins would be "adversely affected physically or psychologically" by having a nyad as a next-door neighbor.

A leprechaun hopped onto the table and planted his feet in the middle of the sizeable pile of bureaucratic blitzing. "They just want us out, Vern. They'll use any excuse under the rainbow, but it comes down to numbers. The more of us they disqualify, the more they can assert that we don't have a right to be here, the more they can fill their quotas with Mundanes."

"It doesn't quite work that way," I started, but a human with rough clothes and rougher complexion spoke up.

"It does for us! We've come here to farm. We work hard, keep our heads low, and ask for little. We work to be here legal-like, but we don't want anyone's charity. And for that, we're a threat. This isn't the first time we Faerie have been harassed, and if we let this continue, it won't be the last. We've been calm long enough. It's time to take action!"

"Yeah!"

The mob started brewing ugly. Problem was, I wasn't feeling too pretty myself. It wasn't that long ago, as dragons perceive, that the Mundanes had tried to run me out of their world.

"Join us, Vern!" the leprechaun urged. "Damant's having a big fund-raising rally. Lots of press will be around. We're going to make our stand there. We are going to fight for what we deserve!"

If I had an eyebrow to raise, I'd have done it. "Really, you all showed up, ready to bang my door down, to invite me to a protest? What do you expect me to do? Roar intimidatingly? Breathe fire on them?"

Now, their enthusiasm tempered with hesitancy, and they traded glances and shrugs. I guess that was what they expected.

"Violence at his rally will just make things worse," I pressed.

"Peace and patience haven't exactly been working!" the leprechaun protested.

"Setting Damant—or anyone else—on fire won't either." No matter how satisfying it might be.

Finally, Gord stepped forward and threw a bag on the table. "Fine, then! You're a private detective. Do some detecting. There must be dirt on Trevon Damant. Dig it up. Get it to us by the rally. We'll expose him for what he is—right in front of his own crowd!"

I snorted, ruffling the papers on the table. Dig up dirt? Just like that, when his rival for governor hasn't found so much as a parking ticket to use against him in a year's worth of campaigning?

Still, investigation was more my game, and I smelled silver in that bag, along with some gold and maybe a gem or two. "Not in a few hours, I can't. No one's that good, and I don't count on luck. But leave the letters—and that bag as a retainer—and I'll see what I can do about your specific problems and dealing with Damant.

"In the meantime, go home and don't worry. And if you do go to that rally, just remember that any lawbreaking or major disruptions of the peace are more than likely going to play into his hand. Gord, stay a minute. The rest, go home."

Grace had snuck in and kept a low profile while I took the brunt of everyone's ire; now, she led them out with gentle words of reassurance and prayers. When she got back, I told her and Gord about Balga. Gord slumped over the table, covering his face with his beard. After whispering a short prayer, Grace got up to fetch him some water with lemon.

"Do you have a beer?"

"Not for you to throw against the wall, no," I said. "Grieve on your own time. Right now, you need to arrange for Urist's bail, and we need to go check on him and start digging into Balga's murder."

He looked up, suddenly hopeful. "Do you think Damant might actually have done it?"

Then, just as suddenly, he wilted. "Nah, not his style. This is his style." He waved his hands at the pile of broken dreams on the table.

Gord took Coral home in his smart car while Grace and I headed to the precinct. I read Officer Starkey's notes aloud on the way.

"If Damant did it, he hired out," I concluded after reading the ravages done to poor Balga's body. "Bet Santry chalks it up to gang activity."

"Maybe you should go talk to Los Despredatores?" Grace suggested. "I can ask around the precinct, then I'll get some minions and head over to the rally. We might learn something from the crowd, and if there is trouble..."

Grace didn't need to finish her sentence. At her peak, Grace had been one of the most powerful mages of the Faerie Catholic Church. Demonic torture had left her with severe PTSD and a fear of her own powers, but now that she was coming back to her true self, she could weave one mighty effective peace spell.

I liked the idea, and that of using our minions. The "minions" are our own little band of stringers: people of all ages and species willing to do a little snooping, keep a quiet eye on a building, ask an innocent question, and generally do the safer things a dragon and a nun can't. Grace insisted on the safe part, and in return, I insisted on their being called "minions." I want to be the only dragon ever to have had minions.

I looked out the window. It was clear, but cold. I wondered how many people would be there—that weren't being paid. I wouldn't put it past Damant to hire an audience of "faithful supporters" to fill the gaps of those whose first loyalties were to the warm indoors.

If he hired the "right" people, they would be only too glad to push back if our side came to protest. That could be a problem.

"Make sure folks remember to stay calm. They were pretty heated earlier."

"Aye. If I can get enough help, I'll post a couple of minions among the Faerie, to watch for trouble. I think Father Rich is coming, too, so I'll ask him to keep an eye on Urist in particular, just in case he gets bailed out in time."

Grace pulled over, and I winged the fifteen blocks to a rat-infested trailer park on the east side of Territory.

The rickety porch would not have supported my weight, but I saw someone peek at me through the Colorado flag that served as a curtain, so I settled myself where the wind didn't bluster as hard and waited until the hollering inside died down and Josemaria came out. Josemaria was the new Beta of Los Despredatores and my contact when I wasn't interested in reminding them who the real alpha predator in town was. Yeah, his momma named him after the saint; Grace thinks that will mean something eventually.

But not at the moment. As soon as he opened the door, Josemaria said a few words that the saint was probably making apologies for in heaven. "Whaddya want? It's cold out here!"

"Don't have to tell me. Did you and your boys decide to have a little fun with an elf last night?"

Balga's a dwarf, of course, but it's amazing how easy people are to trip up. If he thought I was on a different case, his relief would show and signal his guilt.

Instead, he gaped at me. "You crazy? It was like, f'ing twenty below or something."

"It wasn't. Don't be such a baby. No chance any of your compadres have better cold tolerance than you?"

He blew on his hands, but I didn't think it was a stall tactic. "Doubt it. Most of us were playing WoW last night. PvP—we zerged them. Did a dungeon run to power level some drenai babe. Took out a dragon." He tried to give me a snarky grin, but his teeth were already chattering.

"Live that dream online, meat. Well, there was a big nasty with a dwarf on the edge of your territory, and if it wasn't you, then you might have uppity neighbors."

"Thought you said elf."

"I said, 'dwarf.' Your head's still in WoW. If you hear anything, tell me first, then the cops. Comprende?"

"Sí, comprendo. Can I go in now? I left the guys fighting a Level 80 protodrake."

He left me with my lead as cold as my nose. I debated between heading home or meeting Grace, then decided I may as well try to earn some pay.

The alley where Balga was found was on the way to the Department of Immigration offices. I'd go there first to check it out. Then, if I had time, I might go ask Widow Brody why her late husband's boss was making late-night courtesy calls. Maybe I'd go to the rally and ask Damant, myself. Anything to heat things up.

Wouldn't you know it, but as I rounded the last set of buildings and came to the alley, I saw Candidate Damant's Land Rover parked right in front of it.

Chapter Six: Damant at Death's Door

Once again, I pulled back to observe before swooping in. My, my, Damant himself at the scene of the crime. The Fates must have been smiling at me. We were on better terms after I'd found them a good dentist; which reminded me—I needed to ship them some toothpaste.

The driver's seat was empty, but in the passenger seat sat a woman. I could not tell who it was; she had her face turned away from me. Probably a groupie or his secretary. Damant didn't have a wife or girlfriend that I knew of.

Someone had already made a little memorial for Balga at the entrance of the alley. In addition to flowers were stones broken in half to represent the broken lives caused by her violent death. Damant was laying an iris between each half. Bet he learned that gesture from *Idiot's Guide to the Faerie*. Beautiful gesture of respect, very traditional...if, in fact, Damant were the dwarf mine's primary customer.

He lingered a long time over each iris. I wondered what game he was playing...until I moved over his car and saw the photographer crouched beside it snapping shots. I didn't think this guy could sink lower on my list—but using a murder as a photo op?

I flapped down with enough force to knock Jimmy Olson on his butt and treated Damant to my disapproving face.

He smiled at me like I was a potential backer. "It's...Vern, isn't it?"

The fact that he pretended to search for my name when I was the only dragon in two universes was just insulting.

"Can it, Trevan. If you don't know who I am by now, you don't know anything about Los Lagos. You want to explain why you had the urge to come here with your cameraman? Was it just exemplary of your poor judgment and general narcissism that you thought this would make good print, or are you just posting on social media?"

Trevan's cheeks reddened and not from cold. "As a matter of fact, I came here to pay my respects. Justin happens to be with me because we are on the way to the rally. The photos were his idea, weren't they, Justin?"

While Damant was going on about how he cared about "the tragic event" and vowing to look into the matter personally, I twisted my neck to glare at his photographer. Still on his behind, Justin nodded. Even so, I wondered if it was true or if he was afraid of his boss.

If so, he was afraid of the wrong person here. I gave him a grin that told him what I thought of "his" idea and jerked my head toward the car. Justin scrambled up, snatched his camera, and all but dove in the back.

The woman in the front gave an awfully familiar tut of annoyance, presumably at the cold air that had come in with Justin.

"Sorry, Miss Brody," I heard him say as he shut the door.

Well, well. The Widow Brody in Damant's car—and already going by 'Miss.' Was Christmas coming early? I might earn Gord's pay after all.

"...but this is symptomatic of the entire Faerie-Mundane issue. They've come into our world, taken jobs that belong to humans in need—"

"Mundanes," I corrected. "There are Faerie Humans, too, and you treat them just as badly."

"I reject your terminology."

I gave him a smug, condescending look. You haven't seen smug or condescending until you've seen it on a dragon. I didn't think he could get any redder.

"It's not my terminology. It's not even the Faerie's terminology. Your *Mundane* scientists came up with it. If you're going to pretend to be concerned about the Faerie, get your facts right."

"Perhaps, if you're concerned about your status in my world, you should work on your attitude." Damant crossed his arms and gave me what I'm sure he thought was his "You don't want to mess with me" look. I've seen the look done by knights, saints, and even demons; his came off like a nobleman's spoiled and impotent fourth son.

I laughed. "You really haven't done your homework! You have no idea what it would take to kick me out of this dimension, but let me save you some trouble: You don't have that kind of power. And if you did, you'd be doing me a favor."

Rather than argue, he declared he had a rally to get to and sidled past me. I snagged his arm with my tail. I could hear Ellen Brody jerk forward in the car—and Captain Candids ready his camera.

I kept my posture friendly like. "Not quite yet, Damant. You paid your respects, and you got your photos. May I suggest you now pick up those 'respects'? If you really care about proper etiquette, that is. Coming from a legitimate customer of the mine willing to sacrifice part of their next shipment to help pay for the burial, it's a sign of regard. From you, it's a slap in their faces."

I waited while he stooped down and picked up each iris.

I heard Widow Brody shifting in the car. Anxious to get moving, perhaps? Ah, wait, she'd pulled out her cell phone. I really hated modern phones; at this angle, I couldn't tell what she was texting.

The handful of irises in his hand, he gave me a defiant look and jammed the stems into a can someone else had set there as a vase. I didn't comment, just watched him balefully as he strode to the driver's side and got in. The tires squealed as he pulled out.

Chapter Seven: Cold Under My Scales

Alone at last, I could do what I'd come to do: check out the scene of the crime for myself. Police tape blocked off the alley still, and it looked like, for once, folks had respected that. I didn't really expect to find any new physical evidence, though it was possible I'd get lucky, especially if the police had bought the "gang-related crime" angle early on themselves. However, one thing Captain Santry still hadn't gotten into his thick, crew-cut-adorned skull yet was that, on the border town between the Faerie and the Mundane, you didn't just need different species on your force. You needed mages.

Grace, of course, was the magical tank of our team. I was the brawn, brains, and exotic good looks. Even so, as a dragon, I also had the natural ability to detect traces of magical or supernatural activity. Now that Damant & Company weren't distracting me, I could feel a very unMundane, malevolent something. Too faint to identify, it nonetheless made my scales itch. Whatever had been or happened here, its presence felt fresh enough to have coincided with the time of the murder.

I sighed, suddenly glum. Why couldn't I get an easy case for once? Whenever magic and Mundanes mixed, it meant pain and effort for me.

I hopped the barrier and paced the narrow alley, using my nose and my senses. I really should make Santry pay me for stuff like this. Maybe just seasonal work, though. A shiver ran across my scales as the breeze and a particularly intense shadow of wrong hit me at the same time. Then, I found myself standing in the spot where Balga had been killed.

There was still blood spattered on the walls and detritus in the alley, and from the patterns, Balga had put up a fight. I could probably figure out how many had attacked her (or at least how many she'd landed blows on), but I didn't relish the idea of licking anything in that nasty alley. I saw fresh chips on the stucco of one building, a nice indentation from someone's skull on some drywall dumped in a pile. One trash can was dented, its rotten and greasy contents spilled. And yet, no rats or other animals had come to take advantage of the surprise feast; whatever had been here had been more than garden-variety bad.

Grace was going to have to see this. I texted her.

> That is odd. Father is here.
> We're heading to the rally
> but will drive by after.
> Please be careful.

I gathered my legs to launch myself into the air, but I noticed something in the spilled trash, a dark scrap among the spoiled food. It stank, but not just of food; even looking at it made me feel out of sorts and antsy. Did I really want to deal with something that disgusting?

I shook myself. A clue was a clue.

I hadn't expected to visit the scene, much less gather evidence, but no way was I going to hold that nasty rag all the way home. It wasn't only because of the wrongness of its magic aura; it was gross. Just looking at it made me think of all the indignities I'd put up with in the Mundane, and not just for the Faerie who were my friends. And for eight centuries before that, just for the Faerie.

Could dragons have PTSD?

I snorted. What I had was OUDS—Overworked and Underappreciated Dragon Syndrome. And it wasn't my fault; it was the fault of both worlds. All I'd wanted to do this week was take lots of naps under a pile of blankets; instead, I'm investigating a friend's murder, one of the staunchest allies of the Faerie is also dead, and with the way my luck runs, there'll be a riot tonight...

A chill wind cut through my thoughts. If I wanted to woolgather, there were warmer places.

Besides, Grace should see this.

I went back to the memorial where I thought I'd seen an envelope. I found it leaning against the cross, held in place with a rock—or rather, half a rock that had been moved from its partner. That was the equivalent of cutting the head off a rose and leaving it and the stem side by side on the table. Only a Mundane would be so crass or so ignorant.

Oh, the envelope was from Trevan! Of course! I used the folded message inside to pick up the cloth and stuffed them both into the envelope. Even surrounded by clean white paper, I hesitated to put it into my pouch. My interior pouch was a part of me; back in the day, I used it to carry treasure. Now, it held lockpicks and nasty clues.

I paused, looking from the empty and grisly crime scene to the heartfelt memorial that had been violated by an ignorant politico. Balga deserved better.

Suddenly, I lost all interest in going to the rally. With my luck, I'd probably get accused of starting a riot. Let Grace handle them. Besides, I'd already heard Damant's speech in the alley.

I decided to head to the Colt's Hoof and warm up inside and out.

A blast of warm air hit me as I entered the bar, but aside from a couple in the corner more interested in each other than their drinks, the place was empty. Everyone must be at the rally despite the cold.

I debated calling Grace but decided against it. She'd want me to join them. After my encounter with Damant, if there was trouble at the rally, he'd certainly point the finger at me. She would call if she needed backup.

Charlie was playing on his cell phone behind the bar. Good—an alibi in case trouble did start. I sidled up to my special spot at the end of the bar and ordered a firewater to warm my throat. Charlie handed it to me and went back to his game. I was glad to see the television set to an old Stargate episode and not the rally. I could use the distraction.

I was in a foul mood. I guess Damant's comment had struck a nerve.

Unlike most of the Faerie living in the Mundane, I wasn't here by choice. I'd had a God-given Calling (yes, with the capital C, rhymes with D) that brought me here. Let's just say I didn't get on so well with the locals at first. So much so, they threw me in the zoo at one point.

However, when we'd mutually decided to part ways, the Duke of Peebles-on-Tweed, who just happened to rule the land where the Gap opens into Faerie, decided it'd be funny to tell the United States that they had better keep me, unless they wanted an Interdimensional Incident, (capital I, rhymes with I-don't-get-a-break). His brother, the bishop of the diocese, backed him up. Bishop Aiden takes Callings pretty seriously; go figure.

End result, America and I were stuck with each other.

Right now, it seemed America was going to make me pay for that.

I finished my whiskey, and Charlie gave me a quart of ethanol to wash it down. It must have been left over from the night before. I wondered if folks had convinced Bacchus to leave the fountain running so they could fill up their cars.

The first show ended, along with my drink. I refused the offer of a second round, but Charlie joined me in kibitzing the SG-1 crew as they dealt with clueless natives and menacing goa'ulds.

My mood brightened some. If I hadn't come to the Mundane, I would never have discovered television or science fiction. That was something to be grateful for, anyway.

A street urchin came up and yanked my wing.

Street urchins are a unique breed common to Faerie and Mundane—entrepreneurial kids without much of a home to go to and a willingness to make a buck. I've been told there are more of them, now that there are more Faerie humans (who expect the kids to help support the family), but the Mundane world has always had some of its own. We'd taken some reliable ones on as minions. They're good for running errands, no questions asked.

Like delivering messages, as the one clutching my wingclaw seemed to be doing. Grubby face, ten going on thirty...he probably went to public school by day and was some teacher's pet, but by night he skulked the alleys.

I took his message, gave him a tip, and didn't bother asking him who sent it. I knew the drill: no questions asked.

The envelope had a piece of printer paper with a hand-written message:

You think you're secure here, but you're not immune. Damant takes care of his own—and if you want to take care of yours, you'll lay off. The warning has been sent.

I gave the note the fisheye. The warning *has been* sent?

Balga would not have been a warning to me.

I called Grace. No answer. I checked the location of her phone: our office. I called the office, listened to it ring and ring...

I dashed out of the bar.

Chapter Eight: Fight the Wight

The frigid wind blasted over my scales as I flew out of the bar, but panic and fury had heated my blood. What kind of "warning" had my mysterious note writer sent me, and why wasn't Grace answering her phone? Had someone struck out at her as a way to discourage me?

If so, they didn't know me very well.

The rally had ended. I called up the news on my phone as I flew; it had gone peacefully, with the protestors getting minimal attention.

I went to the alley first. Grace had promised she'd go there and check things out. Could the attackers have followed cliché and returned to the scene of the crime? No, it stood as empty and forlorn as I'd left it. Even Damant's flowers had wilted in the cold.

I flew through anyway and found no sign of Grace having been there. I did a second fly-by, straining my senses for her familiar scent and the sense of her magic. Nothing.

I didn't know if I should feel reassured or even more worried. She could be dropping off some of the minions, maybe Father Rich. She had texted to say he'd met her for the rally, and she'd invited him to dinner after.

Still, I wasn't naïve enough to think having a priest with her would stop a nefarious wrongdoer from sending me a warning. They'd probably think a cleric who was also my friend counted for bonus points. I followed my instincts and flapped double-time back to our lair.

I soared above the clean but cookie-cutter houses and square yards of the latest housing development in Territory, and past some less savory houses to the warehouse district where Grace and I called home. Our own home and office was in a warehouse that the previous owner had expanded by tacking on more walls at whatever angle suited him at the time. From above, it looked like a Tetris piece made of cinder blocks and corrugated steel roofing. A pitiful home for my pitiful state.

Nonetheless, at the moment, it was a beautiful sight, especially since Father Rich's car adorned the parking space between Grace's car and Urist's bike. Marty Weaver's rusted-out Camaro was stationed on the street in front of the house. Marty was our minion-wrangler. At least Grace wasn't alone.

Then, I heard Grace's voice, pure and strong...and weaving a defense spell!

I dove for our door, but at the last minute stopped myself short of crashing through it. If I interrupted her spell casting, I might give whatever she was fighting the chance it needed to attack. The backflap of my wings rattled the screen.

I heard an answering wail, a pain-filled duet of guilt and unfulfilled desires. I froze in mid-reach for the doorknob as the cold seeped into my heart as well as my skin.

Did I really want to go in there? Wasn't I cold enough already?

Then, I could almost hear my eldestkin, Durrehkeh, laughing. *A doorknob, Vurnerrah? Have you become so attached to your pets that you mimic their behaviors?*

What kind of dragon was I, getting all worked up over a human? I used to be at the top of the food chain. Humans, dwarves, elves...they were playthings, mine to reward when they amused me or roast when they got annoying. Now, I'm out in blasted wind, freezing my scales off because one of their mates got herself killed? And about to rush into something worse because *I'd let myself* get attached to one? How did I forget what I was— what I am?

This is George's fault. Magically overpowered pain in my tail! He could have gone anywhere in the world to catch a dragon, but no, he chose to set a trap in my territory. He brought me down to nothing, then convinced me he cared.

A misty voice called to me. *He did care, Vern. The Church cares. We care about—*

Right! Care about what a dragon could do for them. Even underpowered, I'm worth a dozen humans, so why have I been wasting my time catering to them?

Eight and a half centuries! That's how long I've let the pope boss me around. Fight this empyre here, defend that convent there, go over to the Mundane side and let them humiliate you awhile.

What do I have to show for it? I used to be as big as this travesty of a lair! Now, Larena massed more than I do, and she's small for a centaur! Once upon a time, I could have generated enough heat to at least keep me warm until I got home.

Vurnerrah, the voice called, *come in. Help us. It is warm here.*

I should go home, back to Caraparavlaenciana. I could snuggle up with my treasure, take a long nap, and wait God out. Eventually, He'd see things my way. I'm a dragon, after all, the greatest of His creations. I am so cold. I should go home, get warm, and let the sapients take care of themselves. To hell with those that couldn't.

I bunched my muscles to launch into the air.

Heed me!

The voice—no, *Grace's* voice—called to me, her song entangling with the anguished cries. Despite my conviction, I paused, straining toward her song.

Silly creature, she sang in a way that was as much magic as music, *why do you hang onto pride when pride is so cold? Why freeze your heart with despair? Open yourself to love, join in all of God's creation, bask in the warmth of His compassion.*

I shivered. Had I let pride freeze my heart? Was that why I felt so much colder?

Ridiculous. If I was so cold, I should just set fire to a building, crawl in, and warm up. Plenty of abandoned old buildings around this squalor I'd been forced to live in.

Still, Grace's voice sounded compassionate and warm. Maybe I'd just stay on the porch a minute and listen.

Her song wove around the baleful cries, surrounding them and overcoming their rue. And I remembered: George after our battle, wrapping me in his cloak and feeding me himself, even though he was just as weak and exhausted as I was; Clare of Assisi dashing out of the convent gates to stand between me and the Saracens and routing their entire army with her prayers.

Grace.

Oh, Grace, who made every irritation and trial on the Mundane side worthwhile.

Grace, my best friend.

Grace—who was on the other side of the door battling something with her song!

Whatever spell had come over me broke, and I dashed in to help my partner.

Chapter Nine: The Wrongness of It All

Grace stood in the threshold of the kitchen door, her arms outstretched, blocking the entrance with her body and her magic, and keeping a wight at bay. The wight, a dark misty creature that inspired and fed upon negative emotions, hovered and swayed, looking for an opening to flee or attack.

Grace smiled and her voice rang clear, but a sheen of sweat attested to the effort she was making. Past her, Father Rich formed a second line of defense behind Grace, a grin on his face but desperation in his eyes. He was singing "Joy to the World" at the top of his lungs.

Behind him, four of our usual minions huddled together; or maybe "piled" was the better word. They were holding down Urist, who struggled and howled like a banshee. Over his caterwauling, they, too, were singing. Somehow, I hadn't heard them when I was outside. I had to admit, I was kind of glad I hadn't; but flat notes notwithstanding, the concentration they gave the song and the happy memories it inspired aided Grace in keeping back the wight.

"Vern, my friend," Grace sang, and her voice rose in a soaring melisma that would have made St. Hildegard proud. "My companion and protector! How good you are here. If you could help me contain this poor creature? There's a good dear."

Grace actually rhymes better in Latin, and she didn't need to rhyme, anyway; she just did it to tickle my funny bone. Keeping my heart focused on how much I loved her, I swept between her and the wight toward the doors of our lair. The wight made a lunge toward me. I spun and breathed just enough flame toward it to drive it back to its corner. It might be more spirit than matter, even to the point of being able to possess bodies, but it was just as susceptible to fire as the next creature.

Once through the double doors, I double-timed it to the back of the warehouse, where Grace had built her magical workshop. The workshop was a self-contained shack at the far end of our warehouse floor. The structure looked ramshackle from a distance, but enchanted wood comprised its walls, with stained glass windows blessed by Bishop Aiden between them and the roof. If a freak earthquake hit Los Lagos, the entire town would collapse before Grace's workshop did.

Nonetheless, the small building shivered in sympathy with Grace's efforts, and I could sense the flow of magic seeping from it to her. The door opened of its own accord as I approached. I'd never seen it do that before.

On the top shelf inside stood a line of mason jars of varying sizes, some of which had a faint aura of magic. I chose one of the larger ones, snagged a lid, and raced back down the open space, slowing at the door so as not to throw off Grace's concentration. I opened the door and slid the mason jar in the direction of the wight. Then I snuck into the room, ready to drive the creature inside should it try to flee.

Grace's song changed, the language morphing from English to something completely alien in the Mundane world. With the language of her siren ancestors, she coaxed the wight to the jar.

And not just the wight. In the kitchen, the raucous chorus of "Joy to the World" faded into confusion, and I saw the minions stare longingly at the jar. Father Rich took a step forward.

"Oh, no you don't!" I leaped past Grace to land in front of him and hollered, "Joy to the world, the Lord is come!"

Started by a dragon's snout in his face and my pitiful attempt at song, he blinked, then sang, "Let Earth receive her king."

Gradually the others joined back in until the wight could finally resist no longer and flowed into the container. I scurried around Grace and slammed the lid on the jar. Only after I'd screwed it tight, did Grace let her song fade and leaned forward, bracing her hands against her knees.

"What took you so long?" she asked.

I knew she wasn't talking about my getting to the house. I picked up the jar. It was filled with black and gray smoke, but there were whisps in an almost humanlike form. Now contained by bespelled glass, it could not influence our emotions, but only react to them.

I told Grace. "Sorry. I got ambushed."

"Aye, for ten minutes!"

"What?" I looked with new respect at the misty form trapped in the jar I held. How could something so tiny be so powerful?

"At least. You're a stubborn dragon."

We went into the kitchen to check our minions. They were helping each other stand up. They all looked shaken, but otherwise unharmed. They regarded the jar with trepidation.

Marty, a college kid studying for his PI license who'd begged us to apprentice him, stepped past Father Rich and Grace, but halted a respectable distance from our captive. He studied it with horrified fascination. "So, what is this thing?"

"A wight." Just for fun, I waved the jar in his direction. The wight lunged toward him, placing humanlike hands against the glass.

Marty startled but didn't jump back. I gave him points for that. He just might make it in the biz.

Still, he gave me a confused look. "I thought wights were like walking dead or something."

I made a derisive snort. "Did you get that from television, a video game, or Wikipedia? That's the Mundane version. Wights were never human, alive or otherwise. They're not quite spirits, either. The legend says the druids created them to drive their warriors to violence—the original berserkers were actually wight-possessed men. Not good for the berserkers, mind you, and of course, the wights eventually broke free of that control. They feed off baser, negative emotions, and when they find a vulnerable or willing victim, they'll settle in for the long run unless someone has them on a leash."

Marty shuddered, as did the others. Urist, who had pushed away from the group and sulked with his back against the refrigerator, regarded the wight with narrowed eyes. Dwarves didn't have a lot of experience with wights. Was he angry at the influence it had had on him, or was he thinking a little berserker violence might come in handy? I made a mental note to make sure he wasn't alone while in Los Lagos.

"So who holds the leash for this one?" Father asked.

"Good question," I answered.

Marty, however, said, "I have a better one: How come you didn't just banish it or destroy it or whatever?"

Grace cleared her throat. "Ah, they're not such bad creatures. They aren't inherently evil so much as feed upon a sentient's more sinful nature. As a result, they draw out those tendencies—violence, anger, arrogance." She cast a look my way, and I grimaced an apology. "Properly controlled, they can actually be useful creatures. Some Faerie police and intelligence agencies use them to encourage confessions."

She turned to me, "Speaking of, I'm thinking you should go to Confession."

"What, now?" I protested.

She pointed at the wight. "If that's what we're up against. In fact, everyone who works with us from now on should receive Reconciliation."

Mundanes dislike Confession as much as dragons. Most of the minions grimaced, and Marty griped, "I'm not Catholic!"

Grace crossed her arms. "Then you'll let Father help you examine your conscience and receive a blessing. Even without the sacrament, it'll still be a good defense in case we come up against other wights."

Grace was not going to be dissuaded, and considering the magical effort she'd just expended to save our hides, we weren't in much position to argue. Besides, I was a little freaked that I'd been caught so long in the thrall of a creature that fed off sinful nature. I set the mason jar on the kitchen table, causing some of our guests to push back their chairs, and waved Father Rich to my office.

I returned to the kitchen with my soul washed clean, but my mind was still muddied with questions. From the way Grace was tapping her teacup while she regarded our sealed-tight-wight, she felt about the same.

"Whoever sent this must have been expecting to catch you alone," she told me as I took my place beside her.

"Don't think so." I passed her the note I'd been given in the bar.

She read it and shrugged. "No offense to anyone, but if I'd been alone, I'd have made short work of this beast. We're dealing with someone who doesn't know me very well."

Urist slouched in the plastic kitchen chair, his hands wrapped around a mug of beer as if it were warm cocoa. I could see a hint of shame through his expression of sulky defiance, but only a hint. I didn't blame him. His wife had been killed, and the killer was walking free while he'd been arrested. If anyone had a reason for dark thoughts, he did. Still, those thoughts could hurt him even more than usual at the moment. He kept glancing back to the wight. When he did, the shadowy mist thickened in his direction, drawn to his grief.

I made a note for him to see Father Rich next, then turned my attention back to the problem at hand. "Or someone who only knows enough about wights to know how they work but not when they don't."

"And not a lot about how to direct them. So, a Mundane? He'd need some serious connections to smuggle one across the Gap, and a charm to control it. That would narrow our suspects down."

"Enough already!" Urist burst out. "We all know who's behind this. Why aren't we doing something about it? We're wasting time."

The wight lunged in his direction, knocking over the jar.

Chapter Ten: The Dirt on Damant

Rita, one of our teenage minions, squealed, and even I gave a start, but Grace's magic held.

With deliberate calm, Grace set the jar upright. "Urist," she said, her voice taking a light, musical tone, "be at peace..."

Urist shoved out of his chair. "Bury your peace spells, nun! I'll have no peace until I have justice!"

He stormed out of the kitchen. I listened, intending to go after him if he decided to take justice into his own hands, but he chose the intelligent route. I heard him pacing in front of the door to our office where Father Rich was hearing Troy's confession.

"Unfortunately, Urist might not be too far off." I spoke in a low voice as I pulled out the envelope with the fabric scrap I'd found in the alley.

"Think this might belong to Misty, here?" I asked. "I did start feeling pretty crappy after I found it. Maybe I was already being influenced."

Grace reached a hand toward it but did not touch it. She shivered. "Yes, that's definitely from someone it possessed. If this was at the scene of Balga's murder, then it stands to reason those who did it weren't in complete control of their actions."

Like me, she avoided touching the oily fabric. Separated from the creature, it was just cloth, but it was disgusting on a metaphysical as well as physical level. She asked Marty to go to her work-shop and bring back a plastic baggie from the drawer. She had a supply of several with contain-ment spells.

I grunted in agreement with her statement, though I was more interested in the notes. So nice of Candidate Damant to give us a sample of his handwriting. Too bad it didn't match the threat letter.

Grace seemed to read my mind. Once the piece of evil wardrobe was safe in its zip-locked prison, Grace peered at the notes. "It would have been too easy."

"Can I see?" Minion Marty asked. "I'm taking a graphology course."

We passed him the note.

"Oh, yeah. Classic. Even though the author has tried to disguise her handwriting, the hint of loops and serifs suggests a woman who was more used to flowy script than hashed-out print. Probably someone in her thirties or older, then. Schools don't teach cursive like they used to. See how the print is larger and just a little heavy? Whoever she is, she's pretty confident about what she's doing. Damant has a loyal follower. Think he talked her into it?"

"Maybe," Grace said, "but look at his note. 'I'm sorry.' Why apologize for the death of one Faerie as you plan the demise of another? Maybe she just supports his agenda."

Now, it was her turn to reach into her pockets. She unfolded a red-white-and-blue brochure with a picture of Damant smiling and giving a thumbs-up in the right-hand corner and another of him surrounded by a carefully crafted mix of male and female humans from the major Mundane racial groupings on the left.

"Diversity Done Responsibly!" the headline read.

> America has long prided itself on embracing diversity, and nowhere has been so inviting as Colorado. No wonder that the Interdimensional Gap opened within our beautiful mountains. Now, we live among wonders previously only seen in Hollywood movies or RPGs.
>
> But the price we're paying is too high! These creatures from another dimension take over jobs rightly belonging to humans, and they bring unknown strife and danger we can't stop. In the past decade, they have been responsible for…

A neat bullet list followed, with handy photos of blood, death, and mayhem. I couldn't help grinning. It was a walk down memory lane for me. Exhibit Number One featured a dead man with vines piercing his eyes and growing out his nose, ears, and mouth.

Grace pointed to it. "Wasn't that your first case?"

"Uh, huh. A Mundane fertilizer company chainsawed a branch off an enchanted tree, traumatizing its nymph. They ground it up thinking they'd create a new growth food. Made the plants rather defensive, what a surprise."

I pointed to another. "Look here: enchanted gang wars. What do you want to bet that was the pixie case we handled?"

Grace frowned. "When they took the form of locusts and God had me send them to ancient Egypt? I don't even know which Egypt I sent them to. Regardless, I'd think the Egyptians would be more upset than Colorado."

I smirked. "Not to mention the pixies who got stuck there. I don't think Damant cares about them any more than he cares that Mundanes caused over half of these messes, not to mention that certain intrepid Faerie have saved this dimension's hide from most of them."

Maybe I should make our own flyers taking credit for the cases we solved and pass them out at the next rally. Could be good for business.

This flyer went on to explain how Damant has valiantly tried to limit Faerie influence in his role with Immigrations, but what they needed were stronger laws. As governor, he'd work closely with legislation...yadda yadda...and a vote for Trevon Damant was a vote for humanity.

Troy came in and tapped Marty on the shoulder. He tried again to protest that he was a

Protestant, but Grace merely pointed from the wight to the office. With a shrug of defeat, he went to examine his conscience and get a blessing.

"You got a brochure? Lucky! I got a stupid flyer." Troy added his to our pile. Although normally a maître d' for the Los Lagos Broadmoor's ritziest restaurant, tonight he'd dressed the part of a migrant worker: cowboy hat, flannel shirt, and jeans with dirt permanently ground into the knees. Five o'clock shadow finished the look. It was typecasting, but it worked.

His flyer read in Spanish and hit upon how the Faerie were taking slots he and his family deserved. On the back was a stamped note: "A vote for Trevon is a vote for you and your loved ones, even those across the border" along with a carefully worded suggestion that they could make it possible for him to vote in time for the election.

I grinned. We may have found Damant's Dirt.

Chapter Eleven: Blindsided

"Voter fraud?" Grace suggested when I pointed it out. "I don't know. It's terribly vague. Who're 'they'?"

Troy shrugged. "The guy who handed me the flyer just said to go to the Immigration Office and check my eligibility and tell the secretary 'Felipe' sent me. I told him I knew I didn't have eligibility, and he looked at me like I was stupid. I tried to ask him if he was Felipe, but he pushed on. I don't think he'd have said anything more to me. I don't know. Maybe I pushed too hard."

"I doubt it," Rita said. "You can't have been the only one to protest. My guy shoved a flyer in my hand and moved on before I could even say gracias. They were probably hired to pass out the flyers—as opposed to the people being part of...whatever this is."

Urist, who had returned as we were reading the flyer, peered over Grace's shoulder and grumbled, but not with the same ferocity as before. The wight flowed toward him, but with a kind of lazy malaise.

Grace had made the right call, making us all go to Confession.

Troy took up the conversation. "So we need to actually catch them doing something more obvious. Want me to go tomorrow, anyway?"

"Maybe we should bring the police in on this and have him go in wired," Grace suggested. "It might be our best chance to catch Damant at something before the election."

I tapped the flyer with my claw. "If I were playing this scheme, I'd use the Immigration office just to see who's interested. Take their information, maybe check their status, and give them a polite brush off—then have someone else contact them later.

"They'll find you out, Troy, before that happens. At best, they'll play innocent and insulted. At worst, they'll change tactics on us. We'd need a genuine illegal to pull this off, and you can guess how Captain Santry would react to that. This rubber stamp, though..."

Troy grunted with doubt. "You can buy those online. I don't think you can trace it."

"Actually, I do think I can find it." I tapped my nose with my claw. "This one, at least, was stamped by someone wearing scented hand lotion."

"Even if you could get into the Immigration office or his campaign headquarters, I think Damant's fangirl is a little too smart to leave any evidence where it could get tied to him," Troy protested.

I tilted my head at him with a smug smile. "True, but what Faerie-hating thirty-something female have we met in relation to this case?"

Grace leaned back in her seat. "Widow Brody? Her husband died working for Damant, and if he did kill himself, as she believes, his frustration with work at least had to have been a factor."

"Yet Damant paid her a late-night visit, and I saw her in his car this afternoon."

"You think they're having an affair?" Marty's voice from behind us was filled with glee.

"I think she's a believer," I said before his imagination ran off to places that would make Grace send him back to Father Rich. "And I think if she blames anyone for her husband's death, it's us, not Damant."

"Which makes her even more invested in Damant's cause," Marty said. "Gotcha."

We made plans for tomorrow. Rita was going to ask around and see if there might be a migrant worker who'd be interested in making a little under-the-table cash to wear a wiretap and visit the Immigrations office. Marty was going to Damant's campaign headquarters, play the convert, and see if he could dig up any trash. Grace and I would worm our way back into Brody's home and sniff around, literally and figuratively.

Troy would get up early and get ready to supervise a breakfast banquet.

Father Rich offered to take Rita home after she'd said her Confession, so we walked Marty and Troy to the door. Troy handed Marty his keys.

"You know, you should call in sick and come with me to the campaign HQ. You're going to miss all the fun," Marty said as they headed down the sidewalk.

Troy snorted. "I like my job. I can afford the finer things in life, like a decent car."

"Whoa! Don't you dis' my Jessica. She's a work in progress! She needs paint and upholstery, but that engine! They don't make them like that anymore. Besides, you weren't complaining when you drove it to and from the rally, gunning the engine at the red lights."

"I was playing a role! Besides, I was afraid it would die."

"She, and she has never failed me yet. You know you loved hearing that engine purr."

They continued their good-natured banter as they got into Marty's work-in-progress. Jessica needed more than paint. The door creaked like the hinges might give out, and I heard the engine miss the first time Marty turned the key.

Then I heard a click that didn't belong to a car.

"Marty! Don't!" I yelled, but it was too late.

A second turn of the key, and the car went up in a thunderous roar and a blast of heat and flame.

Chapter Twelve: Dragon on the Job

Two fire trucks and three police cars crowded the cracked and burned blacktop of our street, but the worst was over. While firemen had quenched the fire, the bomb squad checked out our car, Father's car, and Urist's motorcycle. The ambulances, meanwhile, had been moved further down the block along with us, just in case.

Officers questioned Rita, who could barely talk, she was crying so hard, and Father Rich, whose stoic monologue added a somber tone to an already grisly scene.

I crowded into the open back of an ambulance next to Grace, who had gotten her hands and face treated for second degree burns. When she saw the car explode, my silly nun forgot she wasn't fireproof. While Rita and Father Rich had run for the garden hose, she followed me to the car, yelling for me to get Marty while she pulled Tony out of the passenger side. The magic woven into her habit protected her some, but pulling out a burning body was beyond even its tolerance. Father and Rita had had to hose them down while she sang healing spells. I thanked God that the pipes hadn't frozen.

All the water in the world wouldn't help Marty.

The ambulance attendant taking care of Grace was worried about shock and hypothermia and wouldn't let her back into the house because he wanted to keep an eye on her. He even hooked her up to an IV—to keep her still, I suspect. The EMTs had pulled off her wet habit and wrapped her in blankets, but she still shivered.

I knew cold wasn't the real reason. One ambulance had already sped away with Tony; Marty's ride didn't have a reason to rush.

Grace seemed to read my thoughts. "We promised them no danger."

I snorted but answered as gently as my temper would let me. "This week, we've seen that walking down an alley is dangerous. Yelling at the wrong person can get you killed.

"Marty wanted to be a P.I. The others joined us because they wanted to make this world better.

That's what Marty died for. It's a better death than Balga's."

She sniffled but nodded. "What if this was the warning? What if the wight was a distraction?"

I'd been wondering that myself. I glanced out of the ambulance. I did not like how the bomb team had congregated around our car. "Probably, the bomb was a backup, in case you were better than they expected. Or it could be two separate issues. Maybe Tony got found out at the rally, after all. We'll figure it out, and then someone's going to pay."

She nodded, then closed her eyes and leaned her head against the back of the upraised gurney and sighed, releasing tension. "At least they both went to Confession."

A voice from behind us said, "Yeah, Sister, why did you insist on that?"

I twisted my head to glare at Detective Vialpando. "Careful, Oren. If you're going to suggest for even one minute that Grace—"

He held up his hands in mock surrender. "Listen. We got time. The bomb dog alerted on your car. Who the hell did you piss off this time, Vern, that they are going after your people, too?"

"Aw, you admit I have people!"

"Yuck it up. The captain's gonna want to know why Sister Grace here made them go to Confession. Normally, no big deal for a nun, but tonight...?"

I grumbled deep in my long throat.

Captain Santry was a lawful-good boy scout who, in another time, would have been the best and worst of knights. Suspicious of Faerie, distrustful of PIs, and bearing an almost instinctive revulsion to dragons, he had taken an instant dislike to me, and the feeling was mutual. I and he have butted heads since he first took charge of the Los Lagos Police Department.

He was also a stickler for rules, a staunch defender of the law, respectful and even chivalrous of ladies, particularly my nun...in other words, the ultimate Lawful-Good Knight in Shining Armor. All he needed was a white Charger to replace that blue Mustang he drives around town, and he and I could have some real fun.

I also knew that, regardless of how Santry felt about me, he had the utmost respect for my partner, and I reminded Oren of that.

"Still don't answer my question. You get a premonition or sumthing?"

I started to rise. "Listen, Vialpando…"

Grace bumped my shoulder with the back of her hand. "Vern, it's all right."

She pushed herself upright, though the effort cost her. The adrenalin was finally leaving her system, and the long, emotional day was adding to the magical and physical expenditures of the evening; nonetheless, she straightened her back and looked at the detective directly. She started to clasp her loosely bandaged hands together, thought better of it, and laid them on her lap, palms up.

"Oren, I'm not precognitive. It's not my charism, and you should know that by now. Rather, after the encounter with the wight, I thought it best everyone have a clear conscience."

"The what?"

Once again, we had to explain about the Magical that could possess bodies and fed off the baser emotions of its victims.

Vialpando listened with a look that said, "Can my job get any weirder?" mixed with a certain fascination. He got into the darker aspects of his job and liked it when he found the vein of evil in even the best of people. I'd say it made him a good cop, except that I would not rate him more than low-average.

He barked out a disbelieving laugh when we told him about trapping the creature. "You did magical and 'spiritual' battle with this thing for like twenty minutes, and you think it'll stay trapped in a jam jar?"

Despite the burns pulling at her skin, Grace smiled. "I take my canning very seriously."

He shrugged. "If you say so. Where's the wight now?"

I answered. "On the kitchen table. It's not a threat anymore, though it'll still react to the base emotions of the people around it. I'd recommend you keep a good distance, Detective. You're as base as they get."

"Sticks and stones, drake."

Grace backed me up. "He's serious, Oren. This wight is extremely sensitive. You should have seen how it reacted to Urist..." Her voice trailed off and her brows knit. She looked from Oren to me.

"Where's Urist? Has anyone seen him?"

Vialpando flipped through the notes on his tablet. "Urist? The dwarf whose wife got killed? The bomb squad cleared his bike, and he took off. What was he doing here, anyway?"

While Grace explained how he came to us for help investigating his wife's murder, I listened for the roar of his motorcycle. Nothing. He had left in a hurry.

I also didn't sense the magical signature of the jar holding the wight.

"He's gone!" I interrupted Grace's explanation. "And so's our prisoner."

Telling Grace to stay in the ambulance, I headed back to the house. An officer tried to stop me, but I ignored him. We'd have set off any bombs in my house, and I was going to trust that the bomb squad didn't blow up our car...at least until I double-checked the kitchen.

The table was empty; the wight-in-a-jar gone.

Vialpando burst in right after me.

"Do I need to ask?" His voice said he knew the answer already.

"Put out an APB on Urist," I told Vialpando, "and then get some police protection on Damant. Make sure they're Faerie—any creature with some magical experience—and tell them a wight's involved. Damant's probably at his office."

His campaign flyer from the rally had bragged about how he was at the office by the crack of dawn and worked late into the night, laboring tirelessly for future citizens. No matter what the truth was, I was willing to bet he'd at least show up today in case any future citizens wanted to test his dedication.

Chapter Thirteen: Vengeance Interrupted

As predicted, I found the stucco building of the Department of Immigrations lit up inside and out, with Damant's Land Rover parked conspicuously in front. I'm sure he had a private spot in the parking garage. Urist's Harley-Davidson was parked right behind it.

How long had Damant been there, and had Urist snuck inside to ambush him in his office or caught him in the car and dragged him elsewhere? With a wight calling the shots, either was possible.

I landed by the car, listened hard, then dashed into the building.

I found Urist in Damant's office, holding the politician and his faithful assistant, Widow Brody, at bay. Urist cradled the unopened jar of wight in one arm. He hadn't opened it to let the wight take control of him. That surprised me almost as much as the gun he had pointed at the others.

Expediency? More likely, he'd decided Damant wasn't worth the effort or honor of a dwarven-style execution.

Damant gave me a quick pleading glance before looking behind me—for the police, most likely, though I wouldn't put it past him hoping some humans would come to his rescue instead of me. Ellen Brody, however, kept a fearful gaze on the dwarf.

"Hey, Urist," I coaxed. "How about putting that piece down? Killing Damant won't bring Balga back, and a standoff won't help anything."

Urist didn't look at me as he spoke. Too bad. I could have been fast enough to take advantage of his distraction. "You want to help, Vern? Get the cops over here before I get tired of waiting. And the press. Seems Damant has chosen to risk his life over his reputation and won't make the call himself."

Damant put on a smile he probably thought looked reassuring, but it came off as condescending. He took a step forward. "Urist...it is Urist, right? Urist, you're not a killer. I'm sure if we could just discuss this over a beer..."

His speech ended with a yelp as Urist pulled the trigger and the shot whizzed past his shoulder to take out the head of some civics trophy sitting on the bookshelf behind them. Ellen Brody shoved in front of Damant, shielding him with her body, but I knew Urist had missed on purpose.

In Urist's other grip, the wight twisted and flowed inside the jar, surging toward the politician then back to the dwarf.

"The only noise I want out of your minehole is your confession; and for that, we wait for the police. Or the press. Frankly, I don't care, as long as you are ruined!"

Damant opened his mouth to speak but shut it as Urist twitched his gun at him.

I guessed what he planned to say, and since it made good sense, I voiced the thought. "Urist, you're going to ruin yourself, too. The police are on the way. Give me the gun, and we can keep these two here until the cops arrive. Don't make this harder than it is. You think Balga would want you in jail?"

"Balga is dead!" Urist shouted with such force the wight jerked, nearly toppling the jar out of his grasp. Ellen Brody gave a little shriek.

Curious. Why would she do that?

I realized—she was watching the jar and not the dwarf.

"Balga is dead," Urist repeated. "So why does what she would have thought matter? She wanted to confront Damant from the very beginning. She wanted to report him to the authorities, but I said no. I wanted to keep my head down and mine my rocks. It was our dream. Our own mine, working together, breaking the rocks side by side. And now, she's dead! Who cares if I go to jail? I'm a dwarf. Without her, who cares about a mine? I can break rocks anywhere!"

Damant cleared his throat. "The American penal system is more humane and enlightened..."

"Shut up!" we both snapped at Damant, but my attention had focused on his human shield. Ellen may have thrown herself in front of him to protect him from bullets (and he continued to half-crouch behind her, I noticed), but she kept her eyes on that jar.

Looks like I was on target with my guess about who had threatened me and mine this evening.

I felt some uniquely dragon chemical reactions start in the organ behind my stomach, but I controlled my fire. Poetic as it would be, I lived in the Mundane world and adhered to Mundane laws. Unlike Urist, I was not going to ruin my life to enact revenge on a couple of humans that weren't worthy of the honor of Death by Dragon, anyway.

I would make sure they saw justice, however.

Sirens had started wailing outside. The police had finally arrived. I heard footsteps running up the stairs, and more stealthy ones outside. There'd soon be one, maybe two snipers with their rifles trained on Urist through the window. Santry wasn't an idiot, and Damant was too high-profile to take chances with.

Which meant this might be my last chance to get everyone out of this safely and have justice satisfied.

"Hey, Urist, why don't we just take a step back?" I suggested with a slight jerk of my head toward the window.

Quick on the uptake, he made a casual shift in position to get out of line-of-sight of the window while I continued. "The police are here. I'm pretty sure we can convince them to let us take all this downtown for a nice little talk, maybe open up that jar."

"No!" Ellen shrieked, drawing all our attention.

Urist glowered, no doubt thinking she was just protecting her boss. Damant looked confused at her outburst. Maybe he didn't have anything to hide after all, or so much arrogance he didn't think an interrogation was a threat. As for me: suspicion confirmed. She knew exactly what was in that jar and had a fair idea what it could do.

The police pounded up behind me, but I stood in the doorway. Thanks to St. George, I wasn't much more than pony sized, but I could take up space. I waited until I smelled Vialpando's coffee-and-Marlborough breath, and shuffled enough so he could see the scene in the office. I tapped his shoulder with my tail and pointed to the jam jar Urist held.

Meanwhile, I said, "What's the matter, Ellen? Don't like it when your playthings end up in someone else's sandbox?"

Her eyes flashed—she knew I was onto her—but she recovered fast. "We're the victims here! He's the one holding us at gunpoint. Why aren't you doing something?"

That last, I'm sure, was for the policemen behind me, yet her eyes stayed on that jar.

"Yeah, Detective Vialpando, maybe we should do something," I suggested. "I have a nun with some experience dealing with wights. Not that she really needs one; she's got her own little truth spell."

"This is ridiculous!" Damant finally blustered. "I've done nothing wrong."

"You killed my wife!" Urist shouted. The wight in the jar started to swirl and throw itself against the glass.

The wight shook so hard, the glass jumped.

Chapter Fourteen: Good Intentions

The jar shook violently in Urist's grip, but he ignored it.

"Urist..." I warned, but the shouting had begun.

"I didn't kill your wife!" Damant protested, actually daring to step to one side of Ellen's body block.

Like a basketball player, she sidled between him and the dwarf. "Don't say anything, Damant. You don't owe them any explanations."

"Explanations for what?" Vialpando wondered. His voice held an edge. Glad to know he picked up on what she hadn't quite said, and that he was adding to the pressure. I love putting humans under pressure. And I even got to play Bad Cop.

"What are you sorry for, Trevon?" I asked. "Your note said, 'I'm sorry.' Was that just political posturing, or do you feel guilty about something?"

"I didn't kill her! I didn't kill anyone." His voice shook.

Urist's didn't. "Liar! You may not have beaten her yourself, but it was your men, wasn't it? Wasn't it?"

Ellen called for him to shut up and again protested that Damant was the victim here.

I tsked. "Ellen, it's so cute how you cover for him. Yes, poor defenseless Trevan. You do so much for him. Doesn't he press know about his faithful, behind-the-scenes enforcer?"

"Shut up, you beast!"

"Oh, did I hit a nerve? Could it be even Trevan doesn't know how much you do, the lengths you'd go to," I mused aloud. "Tell me, Ellen, what couldn't your husband do?"

"Shut up, you monster!"

I love it when the villainess's eyes get all big and whale-like. Might not need the truth spell after all.

"What are you going on about, Vern?" Vialpando asked. "What's this got to do with Brody?"

"Guster was all about fighting for the little man, whether pixie or centaur. Damant made his work a living hell, but he had his minor victories. I don't think his job drove him to depression. But I do have to wonder how his need for medication coincides with a certain creature being smuggled through the Gap."

"What?" both Damant and Vialpando asked, but Urist looked at the jar in his arms with new interest.

"Don't you know what they used to call schizophrenia before modern science? Possession. Did you know that, Ellen? Or was it coincidence that, thanks to the Faerie, you found a convenient means for getting a Guster-sized obstacle out of Trevan's and your way without hurting anyone's precious rep."

"Shut up! Trevon, don't listen," Ellen pleas signaled two things: her guilt and my earning Gord's pay. Time to gather the garbage.

"See that shadow in the jar, Trevon? That's a handy little Faerie creature well known for invading souls, even innocent ones with the right coaxing. I'm sure it found plenty in Guster to keep it well-fed, what with his frustration about working for you and his grief over his marriage falling apart—oh, that would be because of you, too, wouldn't it?"

"We haven't! I didn't—I wouldn't!"

"Of course not," I soothed. "You wouldn't dream of doing anything scandalous, especially with Governor Diaz's people watching you so closely, just hoping for dirt. It's not been easy, has it, running against a Black Hispanic woman where the minority vote is so vital? And you being from the Department of Immigrations, at that!

"Maybe, if you'd been in a larger town, Colorado Springs or even Pueblo, you could score some real points, especially with your open borders stance; but here in Los Lagos, home of the Gap between the Faerie and the Mundane, you've got the wrong crowd. The Faerie aren't so easily swayed by political promises. And let's face it: you don't like us much anyway.

"You discovered you weren't alone in that. There are plenty of people here in Los Lagos, and across the state, who aren't too keen on having their 'talking animals' outside of television.

"And magic? Fine in the imagination, but reality makes one big, dangerous mess, right? Why not play off that paranoia, while protesting that you're the good guy looking out for the rights of all the—quote—*real* humans? You could write your ticket to the governorship."

I took a step forward, pressing my advantage. "So why apologize for the death of a dwarf you didn't much like, one with a secret that could ruin you?'

Again, Damant blustered about how he'd never killed anyone, not even ordered anyone killed. Ellen snapped at me to shut my monstrous mouth and snarled at the police to do something about me. For a wonder, Vialpando just shrugged. Good Cop was never his strong suit, but here he was, playing it like an expert thespian.

Still, he asked, "You going to get to the point, dragon, or is this going to take an Elven minute?"

"I don't think Damant killed anyone, not directly. His style is bureaucratic stonewalling and officious threats. Someone else was going to have to do his dirty work: send some letters to make sure the 'right' people got jobs at a local mine, tweak some paperwork in someone's favor, maybe even get her hands dirty with Faerie magics. Fight fire with fire, right?

"And here's the lovely Ellen, his very own bodyguard. Easy on the eyes, but even better: hopelessly devoted to Damant's agenda. Someone with tastes that a double government salary barely supported, but as the governor's wife? Expectations would have to be met, after all."

I paused for dramatic effect, then continued. "What couldn't Guster do, Ellen? Couldn't he bring himself to turn his wife in—or couldn't he fight the wight inside him long enough to get the evidence together?"

During my monologue, Urist had lowered his gun and relaxed the arm cradling the now-vibrating jar o' wight. But as I paused, hoping for a response—perhaps even a confession—from Widow Brody, he stepped forward.

"Damant didn't send the wight after Balga?"

"He's innocent!" Ellen cried. "He didn't know anything about the wight!"

"Ellen, what have you done?" Damant asked. "You've ruined me!"

She turned to plead with him, but he pushed himself away.

Urist raised his gun.

He stood in sight of the window.

Chapter Fifteen: The Dragon's a Hero…Again

I didn't bother with the prerequisite dramatic yet ineffective shout. I'd done that already today and a friend was dead. Instead, I leaped in Urist's direction. His gun went off as I crashed into him, almost in time with the cracks of the sniper rifles from the next building. I knocked him askew, even managing to keep myself out of both bullets' trajectories for once.

Dragon: 2, Cliché: 0.

The jar was flung from his grasp. A third bullet hit it, shattering the glass.

And Cliché picks up the rebound.

The wight hovered only a moment before rushing to the darkest soul in the room. Ellen arched and let out a rasping gasp as it entered her. The police froze in surprise—Dragon: 2, Cliché: 2—but Urist and I lunged for her as she dove for Urist's dropped gun.

We collided, sending the gun spinning toward Vialpando. After a brief struggle, I ended up on top of the pile. Widow Brody resisted with super-human strength, but even a berserker can't do much with 850 pounds of dragon pinning her down.

Dragon for the win!

Ellen raved while the police moved in. Two put Urist in cuffs while a third hesitated by Damant. Vialpando raised a brow at the politician. "You can come in quietly for questioning."

Ellen screamed. "No! He's innocent! You can't do this! Leave him alone!"

She actually heaved her body up with enough force, I nearly spilled off. One uniformed cop with some sense snagged her arms in an immobiliza-tion hold.

EMTs rushed into the room. Santry must have sent them in anticipation of bloodshed. At my sug-gestion and Vialpando's nod, they pumped the possessed paramour with enough sedatives to knock out Andre the Giant. It calmed her, but didn't stop her jabbering; rather, it made her soppy. She lurched away from the cops before they could fully cuff her and threw herself into

Damant's arms, whacking his shoulder with the handcuff swinging off one wrist.

"Trevan, I love you. Don't let anything stop you. Disavow me! Throw me under the bus, please!"

As gently as he could, he peeled her off of him and let the cops carry her away. What a guy.

Still, he caught Vialpando's sleeve before he left. "Be easy on her. I'll send my best lawyers straight away. After all, her intentions were good."

Naturally, everyone got a ride to the police station except me. Still, that meant I could go by air and arrive ahead and let Santry know what to expect.

"A wight?" McConkey said. He'd popped in to deliver mail and stayed to listen despite Santry growling for him to get out. "Oh, Captain, that's a might serious thing, that is. You'll be wanting some strong, burly types. I'd suggest—"

Santry reached under his desk for the oatmeal box. McConkey blipped away without argument. Then Santry called for two of his strongest officers to meet the Widow Brody at the door.

"How do we get the wight out of her?" he asked me. "Can Sister Grace do it?"

"I already called her," I said. "Let's talk compensation before she arrives."

Grace drove over in our car. I guess the bomb squad cleared it. She followed Widow Brody's jailers into an interrogation room. An hour later, she emerged with the wight back in the jar.

Santry took one look at her and had a uniform with an SUV drive us home.

"Get the car tomorrow," he said, and she didn't have the energy to fight about it.

Grace set the jar with the wight in a cooler she'd brought with her, cushioned it with an emergency blanket, then secured the cooler beside her with a seatbelt. She wasn't taking any chances of it getting loose.

I climbed into the back and stuck my head between the seats beside her. "Ellen admitted setting the wight loose on her husband," Grace said sadly.

"At least we know what drove him to shoot himself."

Her mouth twitched in a small smile. "God always knew. But I admit, I'm less worried about the state of his soul now. Not that we'll be praying any less for him, mind."

"Yes, Sister Grace," I sing-songed, and she snorted.

On the way home, I told Grace what had happened with Urist, and that I'd called Gord to find him a good lawyer.

At home, Grace didn't bother going up the stairs but curled up in my nest of mattresses and fell asleep with her head on my flank. She was still snoring when I awoke the next morning.

Two days later, Grace sang the funeral Mass for Guster Brody, which, thanks to the absence of his bigoted wife, was packed with a mix of Faerie and Mundanes. But not a single reporter or news crew. Watching the crowds, I had to wonder why.

The funeral home had written directions to take Brody's casket immediately after the funeral for a private burial. Leaving Grace to clean up from the funeral, I headed home and scrolled the news sites.

Wouldn't you know? Damant was having a press conference, at the cemetery no less, where he had just "completed the tragic duty of burying his friend and—no, not employee, not a subordinate, but a long-admired coworker—alone." Never mind the funeral Mass where a packed church of Faerie and Mundanes prayed for his soul.

Private burial—ha! I could guess the story. Ellen was probably insisting that Damant had nothing to do with the entire scandal except as an innocent bystander, which let him go free. In return, Damant was upholding her wish that all immigrants from Faerie, human or otherwise, be banned from her husband's gravesite, and he used his political pull to get the "story" moved there.

He thought he was coming out ahead, but this was just a reprieve. I and my minions were not going to rest until we found something—anything—against him. If it wouldn't work in court, then we'd give it to his political opponent. I might even swallow my pride and pass it to the *Gazette*. Nothing made McGrue happier than a scandal, and since her Pulitzer nomination, which was also thanks to me, she was a little more receptive to my assistance.

As Damant blathered on to the TV anchor, the camera focused on Brody's gravesite in the distance, and I saw an eclipse of luna moths hovering over the freshly piled dirt. Good move, McConkey.

Just as I'd started to feel kind of warm and fuzzy inside, the news wrecked it by returning to Damant "candidly discussing" Widow Brody's breakdown.

"Once again, we see why opening Earth's borders to the non-human—pardon me, non-Terran—element was such a bad idea. We must limit the Faerie presence. No one is ready to deal with the ramifications, and we continue to see the aftermath of the rash policies that let these out-of-place creatures into our rightful..."

The doorbell rang. Grateful for the interruption, I left the computer with Damant blathering some platitudes that sounded straight from his campaign speech.

The FedEx guy was used to our neighborhood. He didn't even blink as he held out a thick electronic pad and a rubber nub for me to use on my claw to scrawl my signature. He handed me a huge envelope. It was addressed from Guster.

I didn't bother with anthropomorphisation. As soon as I'd shut the door, I tore open the package with my teeth and spread the contents out on the floor to read. There were several thin manila envelopes, marked with names: Urist & Balga, Coral, some others. I pulled over the page addressed to Grace and me. It was dated two days before his death and written on paper from a lawyer's office in Canon City. The handwriting was shaky, but clear enough.

If you're getting this, I'm dead. I wish I understood what's come over me. Most days, I'm so heavy with despair, or so full of anger... I don't understand. It's hard to concentrate, but I can't let this thing beat me. I can't stop until I've made right what my boss—what my own wife—have made wrong. But I don't know if I can make myself do anything about it. Maybe it doesn't mean anything, anyway.

No, I can't let myself believe that. I will do the right thing. If not now, then after my death.

Grace, Vern, this is all I could dig up: phone records, files, some emails I found on Ellen's computer that she thought she'd deleted. You'll see. When Trevon couldn't stop me with regulations, he was able to call in "favors." Where favors didn't work, Ellen did. I don't understand what happened to her. When the Gap opened, our world changed, and so did she. But my feelings never did. I loved her.

The next line was written in large, even shakier letters: ***I still love her***.

I don't know how much longer I can fight this. I don't even know if I should. There are days when I see her and Damant, laughing together. And I just...

I bought a gun. I don't remember doing it. But I heard them laughing and then the gun was in my hand...

I love her.

I gathered my papers and fled here. If anything happens to me, Jensen & Jensen will get this to you. I pray I can find the courage to see this through. I pray I can fight the dark urges inside me. But if I can't... I'd rather die than hurt her. I pray God will forgive me.

My intentions are good, but we all know where good intentions lead, right?

"Not in your case, Guster," I whispered. "Not in your case."

Do you love Vern?

Please take a few minutes to leave a review. Don't know what to say? Say why you liked Vern in this one. (You know he loves that.) Tell us if you figured out the mystery. Did you like how it ended? Twenty words is all you need. It helps readers and helps with Amazon ratings which makes author and dragon happy.

If you want to keep up with Vern's and my adventures in person and on print, sign up for my newsletter at http://sendfox.com/fabianspace.

Acknowledgements

I really should learn to take better notes on the stories I write.

This one I do remember was a by-request for the inaugural issues of *Midnight Diner*. So I definitely have to thank Michelle Pendergrass and Lincoln Chrisler.

It was especially fun because the magazine was doing a Kickstarter campaign and we sold one of the characters. I wish I could remember the name of the person who bid on it, but if I recall correctly, he got to name Urist the dwarf.

At any rate, I had a lot of fun, made a little money, got some Vern love, and then forgot all about this story until recently when I was looking over old stories to republish.

I'd forgotten how much I loved this one, especially the wake scene where the dwarves are drinking ice water instead of beer to mourn their friend. I think my husband, Rob, helped me come up with that.

For those that remember the story from the *Midnight Diner*, you'll see I added a few more details and edited it a bit, but it's pretty much the same. It was a solid story. And just like when I wrote it, the ending made me cry a little.

I'd like to thank my beta readers, K. Ann Seton and Corinna Turner. They caught typos and gave suggestions to make the story even stronger.

Finally, so many thanks to my amazing cover artist, Dawn Grimes. I had a clear idea of what I wanted on this cover and tried to do it myself. The result was laughable at best. Dawn took it and made it into something mysterious and a little creepy. (I'll show you on my newsletter. The difference between a professional and an amateur is amazing!)

There's More Fun in FabianSpace!

DragonEye Series
Science Fiction

Space Traipse: Hold My Beer

The Old Man and the Void

Dex's Way

Discovery

The Rescue Sisters short stories

Fantasy

Mind Over Mind

Mind Over Psyche

Mind Over All

Hilarious Horror

Neeta Lyffe, Zombie Exterminator, in Zombie Death Extreme!

Neeta Lyffe in I Left My Brains in San Francisco

Neeta Lyffe in Shambling in a Winter Wonderland